Nelish Daring Quests

By

Kevin D. Grant

Book 1

Text and character illustrations produced by Kevin David Grant. Illustrations and cover digitally enhanced by April Bodi.

This book is published by Kevin David Grant and KDP publishing.

Printed by CreateSpace.

Acknowledgements

There are so many people I would like to thank for making my dreams of this book a reality. First and foremost, I would like to thank my family, relatives, friends, and members of the 912 community for keeping me grounded. You helped made me who I am today, in which I am forever grateful.

Special thanks to the individuals that help brought my ideas to life. These individuals are Amanda Harrolle (tangible character designs, book formatting, friendship and guidance); April Bodi (graphic design enhancement and friendship); Perfect Printing (embroidery); Eric Quzack (logo design assistance); and Mia Darien for your (editing efforts).

Thanks to John McIver, Gloria McIver, Leroy Smith, Michael A. Rosado, Carolyn Mendenhall, Jonathan Mashack, William Vega, Christian Charles, Patric Sieben, Alie Sieben, Kristyl Tift, Darlene Shaw, Tina Catchings, Anthony McIver, D'Shon Wilson, & Gregory Williams for sharing your knowledge and hospitality. Thanks to my in-laws for your support.

Thanks to my colleagues Latoya Hicks, J'Metria Anderson, and Rose Warner, for providing me inner strength.

Thanks to my readers who provided valuable knowledge, insight and/or support: Deborah Ware, Barbara Delac, Jessica Burgess, Latifah Long, Joell Greco, Martha Rakes, Janet Drummond Robinson, Lissette Kimbrough, Anthony Rodriguez, Germaine Johnson, Robin Johnson, Aisha Nicole, Carol Hood-Venerables, Mr. Venerables, Keisha Grant, Patrice Kelly, SueAnn Hollowell, Michelle Wong, Tionna Richardson Wright, Kim Darby, Harold F. Hilliard, Cynthia Pitts, Candice Grant, and my future support team-

You! I received numerous feedbacks from a multitude of friends of every facet, in which I am truly honored.

Last, but certainly never least, words can never express my love and immediate family support from my lovely wife Candice, and my two handsome sons DeMarion and Desmond, in which I am extremely lucky and blessed to have. Thank you!

Dedication

"My desire is to bring quality entertainment into the hearts of everyone by sharing my gift to the world!"

Foreword

Throughout the ages, life has existed in opposites of sharp contrasts, such as water and land; man and beast; fire and ice; pen and sword; predator and prey. In the ideal focus of predator and prey lies the focus of dominating will. Throughout eras of the past, present, and future, there will always be an underlying nature that will impose its will, which in return will cause the balance of life to be controlled by the superior. That "balance," known as domination, is an inherent, aggressive trait that instills confidence in the aggressor to attack and force the inferior to succumb. Although the aggressor appears to have security, dominion, and possession over their surroundings, it may in fact be the total opposite. It may have been the aggressor's insecurity that compelled it to perform these actions in the first place or perhaps, through its jealousy and fear. Thus, the cycle to impose one's will continues today.

Traditionally, predators are feared and respected by their peers and inferiors, or prey. The higher the predatory hierarchy, usually the less imposing threats and dangers these predators face. Inherently, predators and prey realize the advantages of acquiring this acceptance, and they would go to the great depths to receive such privilege. Acquiring the status as mascot of an area in this world provides rights to either usurp or abuse authority. Fast forward to today's society and the traditional behavior of the superior, dominating the inferior, ideally seems to take place...until now.

There lies a hero that wants to make a change in the "traditional views," by not allowing oneself to accept who they are by nature, but to demonstrate who they are by their merit and self-worth. This hero goes by the name of Nelish, an adventurous peacock by trade, in which he is compel to inform others to redefine what society considers prey, to establish an identity for themselves against predators, and not just be accept being considered as prey, but to overcome the opposition and be triumphant. Nelish's reputation begins in a humble village community located in the following:

Malihayah

In the land of Bangladesh, a country located in the Middle East, lies a humble community compose of respectable citizens such as exotic birds, pheasants, elephants, deer, and other peaceful inhabitants. These citizens go about their daily lives trying to build their reputations in their communities, within their respectable families. Nelish lives in a village call Malihayah. (Ma-lee hi' yah). Malihayah, a peaceful dwelling inhabitation whereas peaceful common refugees of the land co-exist together in peace in harmony, is full of wonder. Inhabitants of the land live in homes compose of variety of branches, plants, earth materials, and other aspects of humble natural assortments of grasslands, huts, and rivers. Throughout the vast land, refugees feel welcome, as they are invited in by senior village community members and embrace this new community as their own. Refreshing is the atmosphere here, where the children play and the adults gather together throughout the enchanting land, living together peacefully. Blissful waterfalls, mountainous greens, and various colors engulf the land, appearing as an amazing paradise.

Led by the founder and village senior elder and chief, Mahato, a kudu, ensures safety and fosters peace throughout the community. Surrounding the village are community elders that shoulders the beliefs and livelihood and spirit of the village. "Ha, ha, ha," Mahato laughs, as he behold his eyes of the view of the land. "What is it Mahato?" one of the elders states while viewing the smile on Mahato's face. "It is amazing to see such a splendor and beauty of this place." "Away from danger and to peacefully co-exist as one village, I believe we as a community have done such a wonderful job in establishing ourselves, and to see everything coming into fruition." "Yes indeed Mahato." The elder leader sounds, following by stating, "It has been a vast many of moons and suns in which we've continuously escape captivity, but thanks to you great one, we now peacefully co-exist in our safe haven, out of harm's way!" Mahato follow by stating, "It is my intense desire to promote the land to other refugees, constantly facing threats of other predators, where in which, we shall continue to dwell safely together; but I am thankful for the citizens that encompass our land and continuing to promote peace." "From generation to generation, it is great to see children play with each other, as well as their parents, without any worries or pressures of predators." "The ever green forest, the vast waterfalls, and bounteous pastures, it's simply amazing that the elders and the youth endear the spirit of Malihayah!" Mahato further stated to the close elder, "For we know all too well, what have become of us, so now it is my desire that we ensure safety with our present community." "We are of one family, one mind, one civilization, and of one nobility." "Yes indeed Mahato, the elder states, as he gracefully bows as Mahato hug him and several other senior village members. As Mahato state this, he witnesses the children playing as they came closer and closer to him.

Several youth innocently play along the village, laughing and carrying out fun actions as Mahato chats with the village elders. "Look at these young ones chasing each other. They are playing without a care in the world, and this is my desire to keep avoid them the pressures we went through!" The younger villagers, including Nelish the peacock, suddenly crash together, unaware in front of

Mahato and the elders. "Oops, we're very sorry to stumble before your presence, Chief Mahato, sir!"-Nelish sheeplish stated. The elders began to block the youth in efforts to protect Mahato. "As you were!" Mahato states to the elders by allowing the youth to remain. Nelish respectively responds, "We were playing throughout the village, where I wanted to show my marksmanship skills to the others as they ran away!" "No need to apologize dear ones!" Mahato laughs, as he states, "We were just talking about you precious ones and how we are happy to see you all playing together in harmony." "Nelish, son of Jareet the peacock, I see that you have a different sense of peculiar-ness about you." "There has been many days that I've witness you displaying different arts and tactics." "Yes Chief. All my life, all I ever want to do is sword fight and shoot arrows. Just have fun you and enjoy a little adventure on the wild side, you know? A little unease, Mahato nervously laughs and responds, "Yes I see Nelish." "I see such wonderful talent you have." Mahato soon embraces the youth and state, "Now go along now young ones!" Mahato graciously dismiss them, and held the elders back to talk to them. In deep concern of Nelish's response and wild manner of activity of sword fighting and shooting darts compose of twigs and branches among the other youth, Mahato states, "We must inform our village that our young ones should not carry out these acts and manners of such violence. We as a community must promote peace, not acts of violence. See that these orders are mention to everyone throughout!"

Outside of the chief leader and the elders, are other noble citizens that are well respected throughout the community for their noble deeds; other members which includes Nelish's parents, which are leaders of the village. Nelish's father, Jareet, is an honorable tax-collector, as well as a servant, and priest of his own home. Once a week Jareet goes throughout the village to collect taxes, in efforts to upkeep the beauty of the village. "Good day citizens! It's that time again to keep our village beautiful!" Jareet expresses, as he greets them, while he waits to receive funds. Some of the men would express, "What a wonderful guy!" and other women would state, "Amazing how he and his family sets a wonderful of example of how to carry out daily routines!" Jareet, always fond of receiving gratitude for carrying out orders, appreciates the satisfaction of upholding the highest standards of keeping Malihayah successful. Nelish's mother, Ava, successful in her own right, provides meals throughout the village, clean public areas, and was a caregiver. She is also much respected throughout the community. She admires her daily activities, and is loyal to her husband. Nelish's parents are the model family, along with other families within the village. They are middle class citizens, which always give to the poor and make sure that everyone in need receives aid. Nelish is the only child. His parents always envision more, but the expense of having another is far too great, and so instead, they spent all of their time focusing on his growth and development.

Mahato's orders spread rapidly throughout the village, even so as it reach Jareet's household. "Nelish," Jareet stated. "My son, words from Chief Mahato rang out that you are among the ones displaying weaponry and gamesman ship!" Nelish replies, "Yes father, but I just wanted to have fun with everyone." Jareet, very concerning as such, follows, "My son, you know how we live here under Chief Mahato's authority." "We are to remain peaceful citizens among the land." "No weaponry or any forms of predator activities are to take place here!" Nelish respectfully replies, "Yes father, I understand, but it's fun expressing myself!" "When can I be free to do so?" "As a teenager I feel that I am of age to express personal freedom!" "We are continuously following rules and regulations that is granted." "Nelish!" - Jareet sounds. Concerning about his image he continues, "Your mother and I spent years trying to uphold our reputation, and in an instant, you are ruining it as such!" "Many days I repeatedly told you not carry out such acts of displaying your arrows, swords and spears!" "There are numerous reports citing that you are leading the other village children and creating such chaos, eventually crashing into Chief Mahato and the senior elders!" Trying to even out the argument Nelish interrupts, "Dad, I can explain!" "This is very embarrassing that my household is under attack by the village community!" "Nelish, you must stay clear of such disgraceful activity!" "Your mother and I showed you the ways of earning respect and through hard work and ownership." "Serve your village with pride and you will be noble among others." "Take heed and see that your production outweighs corruption!" - Jareet proclaim. After hearing these words, Nelish, in a look of frustration, respectfully walk away and heads toward his room. "Jareet!" Ava cried out! "Normally words need to be expressed towards mishaps, but you are expressing such anger toward him." "I, beg of you, don't hurt his feelings!" "His desire to experience new things is rapidly coming forth and we too were young once." "Ava!..." "Yes indeed we were, but these are different times now!" yell Jareet, "Nelish has to understand that he cannot continue to show such display among the village." "He is going against my commands and how will the community view us, if this non-sense continues to carry forth? He continues, ... "We must be a loving community and foster a safe environment here, unless predators will sense us out!"

Nelish took the words to his father at heart, and instead of remaining in his room, he rebelliously escape through the window, leaving home to take a breather, outside the village. Walking through the tropical woods and nature as such, Nelish mumbles aloud as if talking with someone else, he states, "Dad and the village rules and regulations!" "I want to be my own individual!" "Why can he not see the value of me and my self-worth?" "Traditions, traditions, traditions!" "Rules, rules, rules!" "We must do things the Malihayan way!" "Behave this way!" "Behave that way!" "For years he has kept his reputation, but I have different desires!" "Quiet before you alarm any predators, he says!" Nelish sarcastically states as he mimics his father's commands. To further clear his mind, he throws stones into the waterfall streams nearby, observing the rippling reflections of Malihayah. Following this he continues, "What predators?" "We are safe here, and if any of them arrive, we should be able to defeat them!" "It seems like no matter what accomplishments I perform, father is never proud of me!" After Nelish states this, he thought about heading home to take heed to his father's lecture, but as a teen, the natural desire to further rebel, he notices the enticing natural habitat around him, and starts to feel the adventurous side of nature come about him. Suddenly, he begins to become one with nature, by playing around with different branches, trying to have fun and be free. Nestling with vines, and thwarting off between trees, he eagerly enjoy the excitement of the refreshing adventures he had, pretending to fight off predators. One by one, he shot arrow twigs with a branchlike bow at imaginary targets in the middle of tree barks. Pausing to enjoy the lovely sight of being free once more, Nelish states, "Aw I sure wish dad can enjoy the wonders of nature, and be free as a *bird*, well, as a peacock, like me!" "How wonderful life would be if you can have fun enjoying it!" Laughing and echoing aloud, Nelish certainly seem to be enjoying himself. As he continues to focus on clearing his mind, in the distance a vulture predator observes as Nelish as he plays on. "Oh my!" "Oh my!" "Prey alert I must say." The vulture surprisingly said to himself as he continues, "If he's there, there are surely others around!" "I must say that I'm sure no one knew any prey is hidden in this great area, I must go and alert the predators at once!" "Maybe just maybe, I will gain much respect for such findings and they will allow us to feast once captured!" The vulture flew away to alert the predators of the sighting of Nelish.

*****story break*****

Nelish the Peacock

Nelish is a fun loving, adventurous peacock, full of boisterous energy, who love and desire to play with friends. Jareet and Ava, parents of Nelish, are very traditional and conservative and more reserved. Jareet feel it was best for Nelish to understand the roles of a servant and produce efforts as a laborer, in order to gain the honor and respect of the community. He believes in himself and his most additive advantage is his quick wit and his influence. He believes that the power of influence is the greatest arsenal and is the key to victory under any circumstance. Taking a stand and defending for the right to survive is his passion. He considers it important not to except being considered prey, due to something outside of his control. Therefore he's willing to fight for the rights of the defenseless.

In Nelish's spare time, he always tinker with things whenever possible, such as assembling wooden reeds as imaginary swords, or conducting shadowboxing by himself, and performing barrages of twists, flips, kicks, and turns. He is truly a fan of adventurous activities, as he collects and creates an assortment of rock pellets, daggers, and arrows that he used to hone his accuracy. Jareet wants Nelish to use his mind as a tool to excel and his hands as the driving force to succeed, as he had. Ava, on the other hand, senses that Nelish is a peculiar child of a different mold and thought perhaps he should explore his uniqueness, but she keep these thoughts to herself, as she allows her son to discover these traits on his own.

Meanwhile, elsewhere in Bangladesh, the vulture arrives upon a highly secure fortress, full of predator panther guards and servants. The vulture arrives upon an outdoor palace full of splendor and beauty. Around the palace, there were prey servants, performing various tasks. About the palace, laid a brilliant solid black and gold hewn rock throne, and on it sat the chief panther ruler of the predators there. "Halt!" said one of the panther guards as he blocks the entryway of the vulture. "Allow him to resume!" The chief panther leader said, as he continued, "You may proceed forward." Trembling and respectfully, the vulture state, "Parag, I have found more prey!" "Off in the distance, I see them!" "Who did you see scavenger?" "I'm always in need of servants!" - Parag the panther inquire. "I sighted members, of the great Mahato, out in the hidden passageways, located in the Malahayan village." "Excellent work, scavenger!" Parag proudly states, "You shall be handsomely rewarded for your search!" Parag continues, "For years, I have been searching for Mahato the great." "He escaped the wrath of others, but will fall at the heel of my destruction." "Since the ordination of the gracious tigers, family of which I respect and revere, to grant me as ruler of Bangladesh, as they conquer other lands and reign as their mascot, I value their mantle sincerely!" "I take my responsibility seriously and as an honor, and in return, I wish all here, both predator and prey, will be subjective unto no one, but me, as their ruler and mascot of this land." "My prey servants here adore me, and my wish to be served and feared to provide and spare lives, will be adopted in their hearts forever." While talking to the vulture, Parag now turns his attention to the surrounding predators. "Panther brethren, usually I enforce orders to be carried out, but in times past, he escaped the sword of others, but today I shall go with you in efforts to retrieve the great Mahato and his family, in order that they become one with us!" "He is worth the task of retrieving, as I've been extremely waiting to challenge such worth opponents nonetheless, so I will dismantle his habitat, bit by bit, until he is mine!" "Look around scavenger. Behold, you see the servants completing my requests. Soon, I shall have a replica of my image for all the land to see. A grand statue of me to be worshipped by all the land, will be my crowning jewel for all to revere!" "I have a great task indeed for Mahato, and he shall see it fulfilled!" "Scavenger, as your reward, you may be free to walk!" "Ha, ha, ha!" -Parag states, as the panther guards release the scavenger to be off his way. Several guards remain behind to watch the fort and prey servants perform their tasks, while Parag and the remaining panther guards left in efforts of capturing Mahato.

*****story break*****

Parag the Panther

Treacherous in his own right, Parag the panther is an experienced predator who is loyal to the Predator realm, but at the same time, he possesses pride and desires the panthers to represent Bangladesh as it's mascot. Although his origin is from Bangladesh, he is not satisfied with the idea of only claiming this land. Instead, his true desire is to conquer larger empires, thus raising his notoriety, ego, and status quo amongst predators. Parag is cunning, witty, decisive and conniving. He is very fierce, powerful and agile, which is why he is a threat to anyone that stands in his way. Although he understands this, he has an ulterior motive in mind, but for now he accepts the authority the tigers allow their panther cousins to possess the power and responsibility to rule as mascots of this land. Parag and his panther guards stand constant guard against predators desiring their mantle to reign as mascot while ruling their prey.

Meanwhile in Malihayah, Nelish return home. While there, Jareet tries to reconcile with Nelish. "Son, your mother and I just want what's best for you." "We want you to succeed and not face any harm in society." "We are a sacred society of prey that relies on peaceful co-existence to survive." "Remember that my son!" Jareet explain. With those statements, Jareet embrace Nelish and Ava look upon both with a warm and endearing smile. Ava state, "Come!" "We must go to the meeting that Chief Mahato invited everyone to attend."

Although the villagers of Malihayah and surrounding areas co-existed peacefully, the humble festiveness had not always been the case. Within the village and throughout the land, predators lurk and look to conquer whoever came among them. The fear that predators roam the lands always embeds in the heart of the villagers or prey. The end results explain why the villagers remain in hiding.

*****story break*****

Ava and Jareet

Nelish's parents teaches him about safety and to respect that animals of his kind must give in order to live another day. His father tells him to always take heed and willfully comply, and in doing so, he will be able to survive. He had also taught him valuable lessons in that he should remember: no matter where you are in life, always strive for the best in any situation. He also taught him about perseverance and persistence. Nelish's mother knew at birth that he was a peculiar peacock. She had noticed that, as a chick, he sometimes jabbed punches at the air, not realizing he was doing so, but she believed there was something very special about her son. Nelish's father wants him to be a traditional servant, as he is, earning the community's respect through hard work, good will, and maintaining a great reputation. Nelish's mother was sure he would one day become of his own mold, and every so often, she offer some encouraging words that taps into his inner strength. Later, those words perhaps are the very ones that allow Nelish to unleash his true form.

The daily routine of the village includes Jareet traveling around the common areas, trying to collect taxes in an effort to improve the community, or providing aid and gifts to the less fortunate, while Ava assists in providing meals to the hungry and assisting in cleaning, or promoting other activities. Villagers praise the efforts of the good citizens, which promotes positive morale. Youth play innocently and feasts carry on, while stories and meetings take place, which includes plans to improve Malihayah.

*****story break*****

Mahato the Kudu

Mahato, a kudu, senior village elder and chief, is founder of the village of Malihaya, which he upholds the spirit of peace to the village he founded many years ago. Experiencing hardship firsthand as a young bull, Mahato escaped the harsh plains of Africa, while his relatives were attacked and killed by vicious predators. Young and defenseless, Mahato had no other choice, but to flee and forge a new path, or face persecution as well. Throughout his life, he looked for safe havens and one day vowed to cultivate a land full of peace where-in-which other refugees can find a safe-haven free of predators. Immigrating into the lands of Bangladesh, where he realize he was an alien there, he envisioned his earlier dream. Eventually, he forged an emergence and became a trailblazer of his new environment. Because of his strong & majestic presence, wisdom, peace, and sense of understanding, other natural prey and defenseless animals gravitated toward his warmth. Connections, bonds, and friendships cultivated and citizenship began to take place. The village of Malihayah- a civilized safe haven, built to provide universal safety and peace was formed; and thus was declared and named after Mahato. His dream finally came to pass, as he envisioned.

Mahato call the meeting together to inform the citizens of improving plans. Jareet, Ava, and Nelish attend the meeting along with the members of the village. "Citizens of Malihayah, thank you for coming together as always." "Today, I want us to peacefully embrace the moment of our gathering." "Basically I want to inform you that we as a community should remain peaceful and not promote acts of violence." "In the past days, I sent word out to everyone that acts of violence is not tolerated." "We are of one society and we are of a safe haven, so let's promote a peaceful environment to all citizens and future refugees." "It is not my intention to cause any displeasure of our village." "Positive activity promotes a positive atmosphere and I'm calling everyone to embrace this opportunity." "Now everyone I ask, are you in agreement me?" "Yes!" the villagers scream and embrace one another. "Let us go forth and continue to represent the Malihayan way!" Mahato soon left the gathering and retreated to the innermost parts of the village while fun and entertainment occur in the atmosphere.

Meanwhile, deep in the vast jungle and dense underbrush, witnessing the events unfold, the lightning-centered, massive green eyes of fierce beasts, held they stance, waiting to attack such prey as they came within their grasps. Everything around the village seem to be business as usual until this un-expecting day. Suddenly a ferocious black shadowy figure appears in the form of a panther before the crowd. "My goodness, predators are here!" The village elders cries out, notifying Mahato. As a deep, thunderous laughter sets forth throughout the midst of the village, causing alarming panic, Parag the panther unveils his identity as he appears along with his panther guards. Parag pompously states as he commands complete attention of the village, "Behold citizens of Malihayah, there is no need to fear!" "Many days have passed since we've crossed paths." "Fear not!" "I come not as an enemy unto you, but as a loyal friend and servant to you." "Surely I've come to take you to a safer haven, away from other predators!" "Take them away!" he sounded to his panther guards."

Mahato, fully alert of the opposition at hand, as the leader in charge, he knew there was no way of escape, thus he sound for all the villagers to remain calm and stay together, as he realize the time of persecution was at hand. Boldly, Mahato stood guard before the villagers and the predators, while stating, "Parag, certainly you have found me and the rest!" Pleading with Parag, Mahato continues, "Surely it is me you want!" "Take me and leave the others!" "I now go in peace with you!" "Aw, what a pleasant surprise to see you Mahato, the strong and mighty!" Realizing it's been many days since Parag's forces successfully capture Mahato, Parag pompously states, "Finally, I have you in my grasp!" "Now how selfish it would be to invite only you into my humble abode and not the others?!" Panic strikes the villagers as the panthers try to round up the inhabitants. "No, take me!"- Mahato sounded. Mahato's massive size and presence bravely stood tall and heroically before the face of danger, as he shield the villagers away from initial harm. Children scream while mothers and elders try to safeguard them and each other. The male inhabitants try to fend off the panthers, but to no avail, for the panthers capture them with ropes. Mahato tries to invoke reasoning with the panther guards, hoping to divert their attention from the others by allowing them to remain free and capture him instead.

As Mahato and other villagers were facing the opposition, the precious opportunity allows Jareet and his family to momentarily seek cover. Jareet instructs his wife to protect Nelish while he diverts the panthers from their location. Prior to doing so, Jareet held Nelish's eyes and told his son that he had feared this day may come and that in order to survive, one should always respect their adversary and perhaps they would be spared. "Nelish, son this is what I always fear would happen. No worries now, stay safe here and we will sure return for you!" "Hurry now!" After saying these words, he hurriedly instructs Ava to hide the young Nelish while he tried to distract the enemy. Ava, sensing that their time with Nelish has come to an end, hugs Nelish tight and says, "My son, you are here for a better purpose, and now you must find it!" Nelish hid away quickly before the panthers appear. "I'm here!" Ava shouted as Jareet calmly surrenders, as they escort him and his wife away. One of the guards had a hunch and suspects someone else is in the surrounding area. He alerts another guard as he expresses the following, "Wait, I sense someone else is here." "Surely they are." "My scent never fails!" He instinctively tries to follow the scent, as another potential captive may be nearby. "Sniff, sniff, sniff" the panther performs. "Sniff, sniff, sniff. Ha ha ha ha, the panther snarls and states- "Hhhmmm, there is definitely someone here!" Slashing through debris, the panther's curiosity continues to rise. As the panther follows the scent, Nelish quietly shifts and shudders hastily for more cover. "I know you are in here!" "Come on out and surrender yourself!" "Do us both a favor and appear!"- The panther guard states. Shadows quickly follow Nelish as he pace along larger objects and crouches into smaller folds, trying to lower his posture and blend into his surroundings. "I know you are here somewhere, and your luck just ran out!", the panther guard states again. Nelish had nowhere to run. He remain hidden in one last remaining area, knowing that he was seconds away from being captured. The panther guard was extremely close at this point, within inches of young Nelish. His focus was set on uncovering what scent had drawn him to curiously investigate. Keenly focus on trying to uncover his suspicion, he raised a paw and reach in to move aside the veil young Nelish hid behind. "Ha, ha, ha, ha ha!" as the panther guard snicker aloud, "I suspect that you may be hiding in here!" "Let's take a peek here and see what's inside!" Suddenly, a loud command was given by Parag, ordering the panther guards to return all the captives to him, and they left Jareet's estate. The panther guard suddenly disregards his suspicions and immediately followed

Parag's orders. "Aw, okay boss, I just wanted to have fun a little!" Unaware that Nelish was there, the panther guard drops the veil, and went away. He order the other panther guard to escort Nelish's parents away and then he quickly follows the crowd. Moments after, Nelish arose from hiding and quickly went aloft to search for his parents. Fearful of being caught, Nelish could do nothing but remain hidden from sounding forces, secretly as he painfully watches his parents being held captive by the guards and sent away to meet Parag.

Standing in the midst of Malihayah, Parag's forces militarily centers arounds him. As Parag's remaining forces capture the inhabitants and rounds them to him, he states "Behold, my merciful adversaries, this has truly been the day that I reign supreme in the land. I spent countless days desiring to conquer you, while perishing at my sight, but again I say to you that this is truly the day in which you shall not fret any longer. Your ruler is here and you shall now serve me! Pompously pacing around amongst the crowd, he finally squares himself off to Mahato. Face to face, as he sarcastically states, "Ah ha!" "This is finally the day in which I come face to face with the mighty Mahato!" "I do praise your well wishes, indeed I really do!" "Nevertheless, oh my, how the mighty has fallen!....Parag sarcastically states, laughing off to his soldiers. Mahato, while captured and helpless, interjects and ghastly states, "Surely Malihayah will be of one spirit again!" Quieting his remarks, by one of the panther guards, Parag seizes control of the response and stated, "Behold, I am your ruler and confidant, no one shall wonder who their master is any longer…" He chuckled.

*****story break*****

Nelish's parents, as well as the other villagers of Malihayah, had survived in times past by fleeing from the treacheries of Parag's henchmen and other predators. They surely thought they were safe in the discreet village away from the primary boundaries of Bangladesh, the city being very public, whereas this village had provided a safe haven for the refugees. The panthers and predators' primary objective is to instill fear in their opposition and reign supreme over them. By rounding up refugees and dethroning rulers of civilizations, Parag will not rest until his plan was complete. His ultimate goal is for the panthers to become the primary mascot of Bangladesh, although that title belonged to their relatives, the tigers.

*****story resume*****

After Parag finish his speech, he orders the guards to take the village captives away. He stated that he had a wonderful surprise awaiting them. With glistening eyes as he looked into the distance, Nelish watch helplessly as everything unfold before his eyes while he remain hidden from the predators' sight. Thoughts of his parents' influence flutter through his mind as he remembers his mother's warm encouragement about knowing that he has a greater purpose in life and that it was his responsibility to embrace it. Although young and exposed to the harsh reality of separation from his family and villagers, he knew that this moment would always remain with him; as he knew without a doubt that this experience of witnessing the effects of predators possess by dominating prey firsthand, is a turning point in his life.

*****story break*****

Bangladesh

The land of Bangladesh is a sight to behold. The land is composing of rich variety of tropical plants, dense terrain, mountains with lavish waterfalls, and a warm, refreshing climate. The tiger is known as the country's mascot. Although the tigers establish authority over the land, they had given their reign over to their distance cousins, the panthers, as rulers and ambassadors of the land, while they conquered other lands. Panthers are known as powerful, agile predators, which impose their will upon the fearful lesser predator and prey alike. While they tarry the land, they spend most of their time pestering inferior inhabitants and being annoying menaces. They are a confident bunch, who dare anyone to overtake their rights. The tigers have authority and the rights of the land due to their dominant nature and magnificent looks, thus the humans decided they should be the rightful owners and proudly represent as the standard mascot of the land. Knowing this, the panthers adopted the rights and privileges the tigers granted them, as they felt that they too should inherit the land by portraying their dominance. The panthers long to be fear and respected just as much as the tigers are, so they try just as hard, or perhaps harder, to gain the respected identity of their superior cousins. The panthers inherently understand that the tiger legacy in society far overshadows their reign, thus the tradition continues as to why the tigers reign supreme.

*****story resume*****

The captives are taken into the mainland of Bangladesh to Parag's estate, Panthron which is a hewn rock fortress, engulfed with various trees, vines, statues, and river beds. Here, Parag let it be known, the inhabitants of Malihayah village would be forced to be servants and build Parag's throne by solidify it with a statue replicating him, enabling everyone to adorn and worship him. The Malihayan villagers weren't alone. Inhabitants of other locations were captured during times past and forced to serve Parag. Jareet, although captured, thought at least the lives of his community were spared. Parag adores playing with the lives of his prey. He feel that he should be the center of attention, so the slightest idea of eliminating his prey so soon is a disservice and would not suffice. Instead, he prolongs executions by first requiring such efforts from his captives.

Parag states, "Now, inhabitants of Malihayah, please partake of the delightful view as you wish. You are my prize trophies! I shall take good care of you now. Behold the beauty and majesty of your extended stay here in true paradise, along with your other friends!" "Ha, ha, ha, ha, ha!" -he jeered. "But don't get too comfy. Indeed, you have much work to do! The panther family should truly be revered and my intention is for you not to fear us, but to embrace us with your loyalty. You will now show your gratitude by creating a replica of me, as a reminder that I now allow you to live among rulers. Ha, ha, ha, ha, ha, ha, ha! My fellow brothers, show our friends their new humble abode," Parag slyly expressed. "Oh Chief noble one, you may come with me!" Parag sarcastically states to Mahato, while being carry away by the guards, as he was separated from the rest.

Meanwhile, as work activities are constantly moving forward, anyone captured by Parag's forces never had the slightest thought of escaping; knowing the fact that even an attempt to do so was costly. Jareet and Ava knew their fates were sealed, but knowing they might never see their son again, Jareet was moved to go against his nature and try such a feat. In due time, he thought the possibility may present itself. Seeing that Mahato was unable to resist capture, immediately, Jareet thought of a plan that may allow him and his village to be released sooner than expected.

While at Bangladesh, there were working parties assembled to carry on the tasks of build Parag's massive statue. Various captives of each kind led different tasks. The stronger captives constructed the base development of the Parag's fore and hind legs, tail and so on and so forth. Other captives receive orders to perform inventory of material to make sure the construction efforts carry on properly. While others simply made life desirable to predators by performing tasks to keep them happy. During the duration of being captive, Jareet decides to try to follow up an idea by orchestrating a plan of escape, among the other held captives. He knew he had to be discreet and secretive about it, knowing not to distract any guards, unless his plot would foil.

One day, while production efforts are steady ongoing, while the guards tend to other captives production efforts, unaware of outside activity schemes of Jareet, once the perfect opportunity arise, he pull aside some captives of Malihayah. "Listen everyone. Mahato is held captive and it's up to us to try to restore our village. As Mahato expresses freedom among our village, we must try to reason with the predators as well by peacefully asking for our right to leave." One of the villagers interjected, "Our lives are at stake, no matter what we do.' "At least we are together and are co-existing here!" "Let's just remain vigilant and hope that Parag will let us free after we accomplish his task." Jareet follows-up by saying, "Surely we are here up-building Parag's establishment, but Mahato is out of sight, and who knows the amount of torture he's presently enduring." "What's worse is that my very son is left behind and many days have passed since Ava and I saw him! I must escape and try to locate him, whether I perish trying! I have no other choice, but to execute my plan!"-Jareet exclaimed. With a sense of understanding, the captives gave ear to Jareet's plan. "Create a distraction while we slip away."-whispers Jareet. "Best wishes to you both, another captive said to Jareet and Ava. "You there!" sounded a panther guard. "Back to work!" "Right away sir!" - The captives quickly respond to the panther guard's request, distracting the guard while Ava and Jareet began to ploy their escape.

Ava and Jareet stealthily maneuver throughout the fortress, in search of Mahato. Their attempts deem worthy until suddenly, their luck ran out, by the sighting of yet another panther guard. "Halt you two!" "Look as though you are trying to find a way out! "Come with me!"-shouted the guard. To his advantage, Jareet at least had a backup plan which requires seeing Parag face to face; due to the fact that he rarely was visible. Usually, Parag heavily rely on his guards to instruct the captives to perform their duties. "What do you have to say for yourselves? You should have remained at your worksite. Now you will have to deal with Parag!" While continue talking, as the panther guard carry the chained captives toward Parag, remaining upbeat and positive Jareet whispers, "Ava!" "Taking a stand, this is what Nelish would want." "Hopefully we will see him soon enough." "Yes Jareet!" "Our son would want things very much this way." Finally the panther guard appears in Parag's location. The panther guard summons Jareet and Ava to see Parag at once. Ava nods as she states to Jareet, "It is time to fulfill your plan."

Sitting highly on his throne, while overseeing at his vast statue currently being constructed, Parag raise his paw, preceding the guard to allow the captive couple to come forward. Respectfully coming forward after receiving Parag's command to do so, Jareet approaches Parag with the idea. Thinking his plan will come to pass, without any other options, confidently Jareet express, "Emperor Parag, my liege, it would be an honor to serve you by providing for your requests, as you wish. In return, we beg of you our freedom, to remain loyal to you, but from our very own home. Your name and command shall be revered throughout the land, and we will remain in agreement with you. All we wish is for our freedom after all tasks are completed." Stating this, Jareet hope to win favor for his request, but instead, it backfired. "Is that it!" "You wish to leave me?" Parag ordered the guards to bring Jareet and Ava forward as he ordered the captives to bear witness. "Bring them to me at once!"

Parag states, "Citizens of Malihayah, see to it this example that lies before you. There is only one way in, and no way out! At least not alive anyway!" He smiled. "My fellow subjects, I have longed that you were here to stay with me. I bring you into my loft and magnificent home, to live with me and my brothers as family, and yet in return, you bring forth a plan for me to release you? I am deeply troubled to hear such words, and yet, you have no pity for me and my loneliness, should you depart. I have no patience for betrayal! See to it that they enjoy their last breath before their departure!"

The rest was history. The look in Jareet and Ava's eyes explains it all, as they knew their fates were sealed. Although panic-stricken and hopeless, they remained confident and strong before those who watched as they were carted away. Jareet and Ava were no more. The villagers watched the panthers mock the noble couple before their torturous deaths.

"Long live Nelish!" Jareet and Ava shed tears before they were cast away. "Nelish who? I never knew!" Parag laughs, as the guards laughs along with him. "On with it, unless anyone else desires a vacation along with them!" Parag slyly said. He orders the prior inhabitants to proceed with their tenure, while instructing the recent captives to pay attention to their new tasks.

Meanwhile back at the village of Malihayah, many days passed and Nelish finally decides to come out of hiding. (During the battle, while the captives were led away, Nelish remains hidden, for fear of his life.) As he stealthily arises out of cover, his sullen eyes glance toward the horizon. He helplessly stood in a daze, mentally pondering the events that had taken place. In the quietness, he stood there and thought of the lessons his parents had taught him. He envision his father teaching him to work hard and embrace his role of servitude, while he sense his mother encouraging him to tap deep into his natural fighting instincts and embrace his potential by moving forward. While remaining deep in thought, he figure that yesterday was gone and tomorrow was yet to happen, but if he could control the present, then he had the chance to face a better tomorrow.

With that notion, a ray of sunlight shone upon him as if the heavens have parted before him. A sense of self-worth engulfs him as he awoke from his sorrow state and gathers his sense of self. "I can't believe this is what father warned me about!" "Predators should not get away with this!" "I must be brave and go after my parents!" "My village depends on me!" Looking at the destroyed villages and the remains thereof, he collects the remains of his created weaponry as he plans to search for his parents and other villagers. Unaware of where the captives had been taken, Nelish knows his chances are bleak. Knowing the treacherous obstacles that lay ahead, he is determine to find his parents by searching for any clues he could find. The events leading until then had been the saddest moment anyone should ever have witness.

While Nelish wanders the land and look for clues in efforts of recovering members of his village, he notice some tracks. Individual tracks became several, and then several became many. As he follow the trails, he took flight to better uncover what the tracks reveal. As the passages unfold, he heard the sound of a commotion taking place in the distance. As he approaches, he came across some prey as some predators surround them. Nelish moves for cover as he surveys what is happening. He notices several victims being taunted by vultures nearby. The prey included several colorful toucans, some antelope, and a pink flamingo. The vultures are neutral predators or scavengers that annoy anyone in sight, basically harassing and looking for the opportunity to attack anyone. As the vultures spoke with their captives, doubt crept into the minds of the victims, as if they thought they were soon goners. "My, what do we have here fellas?!" –Said a vulture, while licking his beak.

"Food, precious food, I suppose!" Sounds another vulture. "Senoirs, we mean no harm. –sounded the flamingo. "What troubles you?" One of the toucan's states, anticipating the vultures would lose focus on corning them. "Well prey, this is your lucky day!" "We are having a party, and you guys are definitely invited."- Sounds yet another vulture. "Actually, you guys are the main attraction, so why don't you come and join us!"-Sounds another vulture, while laughing eagerly, as they drew closer to the prey visitors.

"SNAP!" Suddenly, a cry rang out from one of the vultures. "*OUCH, ooh, OUCH*!" "*My wing, my wing*!" he yells. He searches for the source of the pain. An arrow made of rock interwoven with thick wooden tree bark is found deeply lodged into the center of his wing. The vultures focused their attention on the area they believe the arrow was shot from. As they look, there arose from the shadows, with a plumage spread and colors fully displayed, a peacock with fierce eyes appears, ready and willing to attack. Nelish announced, "Let them go!"

The vultures, astonished and puzzled, focused their attention to Nelish. They shouted, "What are we waiting for?" "It's just a peacock. Get him!" Indeed, Nelish was outnumbered, according to the analysis of the situation at hand; of vigilante versus the opposing threats. But at the present moment, he feels he has nothing to lose because he is all alone, while in search for his family; he might as well die trying. He feels as if he has to defend the victims, based on his own experiences, firsthand. The vultures races toward the peacock, full of rage and fury; realizing what he just did to their wounded friend. "You have some nerve, attacking our friend like this peacock!" "Prepare to meet your doom!"- cries another vulture while flying towards Nelish. Nelish, in preparation of conducting a faceoff with the vultures, gathers himself, spread his wings inward, cocooning himself and in an instant, he unleashes his position, thwarting several batches of rock pellets outward, reflecting them into the vultures' eyes. *"OUCH!" "OUCH!" "My eyes!"* They cry aloud.

"Don't mellish with Nelish!" Nelish replies. "I'm not sure who you goons think you're messing with, but there's plenty more where that came from, unless you scram!"

Scattered and confused, the vultures blindly runs into each other, embarrassing themselves; as they try to regain their composure. Awkwardly, they scoff loudly at Nelish by saying, "You haven't seen the last of us!" Then they flew off their separate ways. After the scene settles, the witnesses come forward. "Wow, you surely put on an amazing performance!" A toucan states. "Yeah, that was an awesome firsthand view we've witnessed today!"-Stated a gazelle. "We've never seen such bravery before!" Amazed and astonished, the victims praised Nelish as he detached them from their ropes.

As he released them, Nelish decide to try and encourage them. Nelish states the importance of believing in themselves by standing up for what's right regardless of the outcome. "Hi friends! - I'm Nelish the Peacock, and I have joined you today because I saw what was happening and felt compelled to make a change. Predators only allow themselves to be as such because we allow them to behave as such. Today, I stand to make a difference. Not only for me, but because my loved ones and my village are counting on me to make a stand! Should I be alone? No, because one ray of hope can produce waves of hope! You can be that ray!"

The victims were delighted as Nelish spoke such positive words. They were moved and impressed by such wisdom. They felt that his character was well beyond his years. His speech compelled them to be believers of themselves. One such individual in the group was so compelled by his speech, felt he should befriend Nelish.

The flamingo approaches Nelish and introduces himself. "Please to meet you, Nelish. Dominic's my name, and learning new experiences is my game! I'm very touched by your words and it would be an honor if you allow me to assist in your efforts to find your family."

The remainder of the victims thanks Nelish for his heroic efforts and went on their way. "Thank you Nelish again for saving us." We owe you our lives! We will spread the word about your bravery and your efforts of restoring your village. Although we are many miles and days from here, I'm sure aid efforts can restore your village somehow." "We were actually visiting on a school experiment trip performing field study, but ended up cornered by those desperate scavengers." Dominic states - "I'll standby Nelish's side. You guys go back and tell the professor I'm gaining extra credit by staying behind!" The visitors went their separate ways. Dominic remains with Nelish and tells more about himself. Dominic stated that he was bullied by predators, not only as prey but because of his brilliance. Nelish was delighted that Dominic thought it was an honor to join him. He tells Dominic that his intelligence will prove useful and that he should always believe in himself, because he could always be one step ahead of the opposition if he could out-think them. Dominic indeed thinks it would be an honor to assist Nelish, and they travel onward.

*****story break*****

Dominic the Flamingo

Dominic the Flamingo is born to a wealthy, privileged family from the lands of Spain. He is well educated at private schools, where his family sent him for fear of his being attacked because of his exquisitely high IQ. He spends most of his time experimenting with his curiosities, including engineering, mechanics, developing schemes, providing medical assistance, and producing formulas.

Dominic's family line had escaped from the predators of Spain after constant threats to seize them because of their vibrant colors, and being a delicacy to eat. Dominic's family thought it best to allow him to explore Asia and further his development. In doing so, he would further enhance his knowledge and gain firsthand experience to utilize in his research. Up until now, Dominic had excelled with his intellect. His goal had been to learn all of the environment of Asia while here, until he was captured by the vultures.

Dominic is a high character guy, with positive energy and attitude. He's also very detailed-oriented, and pristine. Loyal to a fault, Dominic is the perfect right hand kind of friend and is always keen upon the situation at hand.

As Nelish and Dominic travels, their friendship rapidly grows. They discuss their upbringings, their similarities and differences, as people do. Dominic said that Spain was full of beauty and described the atmosphere as very slow-paced and relaxed. He states he like seafood and also loves to learn new things, but he was more reserved regarding making friends. His experience in another country allows him to express himself a little more. Nelish mention that he is more of the outgoing, fun-loving type, and that he often took advantage to become one with nature whenever the opportunity is given. "The more friends around, the merrier the experience!" Nelish said.

Dominic was impressed with Nelish's fighting skills, and again thanked Nelish for his heroic efforts. He asks, "Where did you learn moves like that?" Nelish said, "Those defense mechanisms are natural instincts, which are counter-actions to others' actions. Basically, I just learned those on the fly!" Eagerly Dominic states, "Nelish, I noticed that you were surrounded by numerous predators, but the number amount seemed to faze you non-the less. Splendid senior! Either you have some special adrenaline, or you have an uncanny fighting ability that cannot be explained. I want to take a good look at you and examine you by conducting research."

Dominic sheds some insight to Nelish by stating that he could provide some enhancements to Nelish's natural abilities, which would allow him to be the ultimate defender. Nelish is astonish to hear such words by Dominic's abilities and is eager to see such works and states it wasn't an accident they had met today. Dominic didn't have much of a social life, but he mentioned that he would love Nelish to visit his hideout. It would take some time to actually develop his enhancements as well as deter him from his journey to locate his parents. Nelish thought for a moment, and then agreed to follow Dominic, because first, he would be at a disadvantage in finding his parents because he did not know where they were located, and secondly, he was not fully equipped to handle the opposition. Dominic led Nelish to his secret hideout and began utilizing his skills by creating all sorts of enhancements for Nelish.

Dominic's Hideout

Dominic and Nelish finally arrive at the hideout, which is found in the marshy lagoons of the *Isles of Nomi*, off the coast of Bangladesh. At first glance, Dominic's hideout appears to be regular land, compose of marsh and greenery leaves. As he approaches a hidden door, he used a secret code to gain access to his hideout. With a push of a button, the greenery opens up into an engineered high powered layer, encompassing an inviting gateway to permit entrance inside. As they enter, Nelish examined the place. It was composed of high tech computers, gadgets, and an assortment of gizmos.

"Wow!" Nelish cheered. "Your place looks like a nuclear facility down here!" Nelish laughed. "Gracious Nelish!"- Dominic states. "I spent a lot of time honing in on my studies and creating gadgets to further my research, so I need further mechanisms to make all of this possible."

As he explores the lab, Dominic gathers several pieces of equipment to formulate his research. Suddenly, Dominic asked Nelish to demonstrate his fighting moves while he performs a full evaluation on him. "Let's take a look at you." While studying his motions carefully, Dominic gathers ideas and formulates conclusions based on his visual analysis. Dominic had noticed Nelish's earlier attacks, when he shot an arrow into one of the vulture's wings. "Ah ha, Nelish!" Pondering the fighting scene that Nelish conducted,

Dominic continues, "I notice that you have a natural aggression to fight instead of producing flight as normal prey performs. I want to perform further research to make a proper determination of your natural reactions. Step into my chamber. Once inside, a series of tests will be run." "Sure thing Dominic!"- Nelish excitedly replies while stepping into the vast chamber. "I want to see what I'm made of!" Dominic continues, "I will now insert test probes over various places of your body, including your head and feet." "Surely this will not hurt right Dominic?"- Nelish laughingly replies. "No worries senor." "I ensure you will not feel any pain necessary. Energy waves may cause vibration sensations while these probes are channeling through different facets of your body, but this is necessary to gather detailed results." Dominic set the components to run an image scan, determining results regarding Nelish's fighting genetic mechanics and make-up. Nelish stood momentarily still as the electronic pulses stream through every direction, calculating tests every per second. A mechanical voice calls out the results. "*Data does not compute. Data does not compute.*" "Amazing, just amazing!" Dominic cheers, responding to the results. Opening up the chamber and clearing Nelish from the testing probes, Dominic releases Nelish out of chamber. "What are the results Dominic?"- Nelish curiously replies, witnessing Dominic's eager reaction to the results. Dominic replies, "I'm astonished! Data analysis simply cannot provide reasoning why your genetic make-up allows you to react opposite in comparison to how usual animals responds to threats!" Nelish responds, "Well it simply means that I'm born for adventure!" Dominic replies, "Si senor! Now we have to improvise on how to enhance your manner of attacks!" "Hhmmm."

Dominic thought of an ingenious plan. He asks Nelish to pluck one of his train feathers, and Nelish complies. "Nelish, with your natural fighting ability, perhaps I can enhance your arsenals by making you the ultimate fighter!" "Give me a moment to demonstrate!" Dominic formulates a solution by adding some chemicals together and as he creates the mixture, he explains to Nelish that he could use his tail feathers as weapons of many sorts. Nelish love the idea of being able to utilize his natural features as an added bonus to his offensive arsenal. Dominic elaborates by explaining that he's trying to perform a specialized bonding solution sequence, which Nelish would be able to pour on any feather to use it as a weapon. The chemicals compound began, drastically changing colors, as bubbles fizz and spazzle. "Okay now the solution is almost complete!" A little mixture of this! "A tad bit of that!" "One more minuto!"- Dominic joyfully states as he awaits the chemicals to settle together inside of a metal pot. The chemical solution is now finalize and complete. Dominic performs the experiment by pouring the specialize mixture onto one of Nelish's detached feathers. He did so and in a matter of moments, the feather was completely hardened. "Voila!" Dominic said excitedly. "All complete."-Dominic confirms. "Wow!" "Dominic!" Nelish surprisingly screams! He continues by stating, "You are truly a genius!" "Keep this place fortified and top-secret!"

Nelish is impressed as he holds the hardened feather into the light. An instant sparkle sheen reflection travels down the feather, expressing the brilliance of how hardened it was. "Magnificento!" Nelish shouted, full of excitement. Nelish begin to thrust the hardened feather as if he was a knight. Utilizing the feather all in one motion, he twist and twirl, and twist and twirl all the more, while performing flips. As he did so, he got the hang of his new weapon enhancements. "Wait, Nelish, that's just one feather! You have many more!" Dominic laughs. Amazed at Dominic's statement, Nelish stated, "Yeah, you are right, but this one is so amazing! Dominic, I love my new toys!" Nelish laughed.

Dominic pours the solution in a vial and places it into a brown pouch. He said that the solution itself would not harden in the vial. Once it's poured or added into another substance, then the transformation would occur. He gives the pouch to Nelish and states, "Nelish, you may use the bond as you wish. Now you will always be equipped with weapons at your disposal."

Nelish replies, "Wow, at a moment's notice, I can produce arrows, swords, clubs, boomerangs, whatever I wish!"

Dominic replies, "You bet, my friend. As you wish!"

As they converse, Nelish begin to discuss his upbringing and his parents. "My father was a good leader and head of the household. He was always determined to serve others before himself. My father always taught me life's values and to always keep a proper balance of them, in whatever I experience. He taught me grace, humility, simplicity, and servitude. My mother was always compassionate. She understood things about me, when father didn't. It was as though she was an extension of my thoughts and actions. Well, that's why I believe they are called mothers, because they understand the true cause and effects of our expressions. My parents stated that they were from the land of India, but they separated from the land to experience life together. They were really glad to help others whenever they could, because of the blessings they received by being in a thriving country. No matter where they lived, they were always positive examples, always willing to lend a hand. I can't wait until I find my parents. I want to thank them so much for always being there for me. Just you wait, Dominic! You will have a blast meeting them! Fantastico, as you might say!" Nelish laughs.

Dominic said, "Nelish, it will be a pleasure to meet them. It sounds as if you have very dedicated parents and that's a plus. Being from Spain, our heritage is all about having fun with mi familia!"

Nelish states, "If Spain is anything like Malihaya, then I'm quite sure everyone has a blast!"

While Nelish is in deep thought, he begins to ponder how to find his parents. The days leading up to this point simply is unbearable. Wondering what the village may be going through at this point in time, constantly cross his mind, as he look for any indications that will possibly lead him to reunite with his community again. "Dominic!" Nelish says. "How well do you know the areas around here?"

Dominic replies, "About as well as my GPS navigational system will allow me!"

As Dominic whip out his GPS, Nelish suddenly has an idea. "Dominic, I don't know where my parents are, but I know there's a possibility that you could help me find them!"

"Maybe I could... Wait a fraction of a millisecond. Voila!" Dominic shouted. "Indeed I can, and here's how!" Dominic eagerly continues, "I can create a tracking device, more like a homing beacon! Once the homing beacon is assembled, you can find a moving target to place it on. In return, the monitor will pinpoint its coordinates, and there the signal will confirm the target!"

"Awesome, Dominic!" Nelish replies. "You can create the tracking device, and perhaps when a predator appears, I can get in close range and fire a tracking device on them. Afterwards we can use your homing signal device to track their movements, and hopefully that way, they can lead us directly to my parents!" shouts Nelish. Dominic gathers his materials and began constructing the tracking device as designed, while Nelish began making his weapons by detaching several feathers and pouring the bonding material solution on them.

Meanwhile in Bangladesh, construction of Parag's image is steadily in progress. Captives receive constant orders to add layers of foundation to build Parag's throne, while a multitude of others are working in groups to speed up the efforts. By the sweat of their brow, they answer orders from members of the panther clan, for fear of receiving torture. Others feed the predators delicacies, fan them, or clean up the province to make it remain presentable, according to Parag's standards. As Parag sit upon one of his throne, he constantly stares at the buildup of his statue in progress.

He began to state the history of his accomplishments to some of the captives nearby. "Ah, my hirelings, this is the life of your supreme ruler. I truly commend you for your efforts and obedience by willfully sacrificing yourselves to please me! As a gratitude for your services, why, I would be honored to tell you more about myself, as I feel now that you are fitting in quite nicely and making yourselves well acquainted!" Parag exclaims. "I have answered the call of leadership, by following my leader's existence before me. I must acknowledge and thank them, through tireless sacrifice and determination. I respectfully carried out the orders of the code and honored the authority over me! As of the present, I have battled and conquered fierce rivals, enforced respect in those beneath me, and rightfully deserve every moment of gratitude awarded me." Parag said proudly as he looks upon the monument's current development. "If only the tiger force can see how we--the panther clan--have established our dominance here, they would be honored and well pleased! I believe it is my destiny to reign supreme!" As he thought of another subject, he interjects, "I need more subordinates! The process of completing my territory is not going quickly enough. Panther clan, assemble yourselves, then go and retrieve more servants." "Right away my liege.", sounded one of the panther guards, as they assemble themselves and taking heed to his command.

As the panthers run off to follow Parag's command, he pace around his courtyard and began developing deeper thoughts of his accomplishments. He eventually looks off in the distance beyond the land with a haughty posture, and states, "Soon enough, Bangladesh and possibly the land of India will honor me as I reign supreme! Ha, ha, ha," Parag roared. "Now make my dreams come true, servants. Back to work!" - He screams.

Several days later…

      Dominic finally assembles the tracking devices. He explains what their capabilities are and how effective the target ranges shall be in a given area. Nelish is fully equipped with his weaponry as well. At this point, Nelish and Dominic are quite comfortable hanging out together. Dominic share many exciting stories from Spain, and speaks of its lavish seafood. His favorite meal composes of all types of seafood, most preferably shrimp. Nelish says his parents always inform him that they had to constantly move for protection against predators, and that predators tend to prey on any species that are a threat to their rule. He continues saying that their moves throughout the land were rapid and the stays brief. They eventually moved away from normal civilization and ended up in common villages, in order to survive. He mentions that his upbringing is very humble, but he always makes the most of it. Friends are abundant and Nelish had somewhat understood that as a community as a whole, at least he isn't facing those situations alone. While thinking of the fun times, Nelish decides to get a breath of fresh air outside of Dominic's hideout. Dominic thinks of a better option by taking Nelish on a tour, to capture all the beauty of the land. Dominic excitingly express, "Nelish, outside of surrounding predators, Bangladesh is very beautiful. It kind of reminds me of my country Spain! The splendor, the nature, oh the abundance of life is ever amazing and fantastico!" "While studying advance topics in physics before leaving Spain, a successful team of students and I often gather in exotic locations to gather specimen to examine our theories. I gladly want to show you a few examples in this country." So he leads the way and shows Nelish all the surrounding sites where he performs his research. As Dominic explains his latest study at this particular site, Nelish hears laughter ahead. Nelish flew a little closer. "Dominic, do you hear that?" "Sounds like familiar voices I once heard!" Nelish states, he continues on by whispering,

"Quiet, while I take a closer look!" As he peers through the greenery, he finally confirms whose laughter it was; it proves to be that of panthers, Parag's henchmen. As Nelish heard their laughter approach, it brought flashbacks of the day his parents had been seized by them. "What is it senior?" -Dominic curiously asks. "I heard such laughter before."- Nelish alarmingly responds. He recognizes the echoing laughs and jittery grins. The time has arrived where he finally gets the chance to see the enemies that have taken his family from him. The moment grew strikingly near. Nelish motioned to Dominic that the laughter indeed belonged to the panthers and that they needed to move above ground and wait for the right moment to deliver the tracking devices. "There they are!" Dominic whispers. "Yes!" Nelish states. "It has come down to this!" "They are the ones who took my parents and villages away!" "We must remain hidden from them!"

Nelish and Dominic quietly flew up to gain a better viewpoint. Out of the brushes appears the panthers, and they weren't alone. With them were more captives, tied together and being dragged along behind the panthers as they led them back to Parag's domain. Nelish states, "Look, more captives, just like the members of my village!" It appears that these predators need these captives for something far greater than this moment! We must not let them out of our sight!" "Please sirs." We are just sightseeing and just enjoying the wonderful view of the splendid land. We mean no harm to anyone. Please spare us and allow us to return back to our lands."

The panthers mock them. "Silence foolish travelers. Your scouting has come to an end! Be at peace with us, for we have many pleasantries for all of you to enjoy!" -Laughs a panther guard. "Parag will be proud of us and maybe we can rest awhile. As a bonus, these captives will spoil us mightily tonight with massages and other pampering. Sure could add some plush padding for my pillows, but their services will do for now!" another said loudly. As the panthers led the way back, they decide to split up. They want to make sure all territory was covered, so that no potential captive is left behind. The panther guard in charge shouts, "Spread out! See that all captives are accounted for!"

Hidden behind branches and other surrounding plants above, Nelish subtly rose out of cover and as he looks upon the captives, in the distance, he notices one captive in particular--a female Sarus crane--stare suddenly at him. He pauses for a moment and as he stares back, he lifts a pointed wing feather in a "Shh" motion with a sly smile and a wink, as confirmation that they would be rescued. He knew he only had one chance to make the best strike, so he waits for the perfect opportunity. "Nelish!" -whispers Dominic, "You have one perfect opportunity to strike." "Once the nano-device unleashes, it will provide a homing signal and we will be sure to track them!" Dominic continues- "Be sure to make the proper selection and aim wisely!" Dominic, Nelish smartly states, "I'm born to make perfect strikes!" As the panthers strategizes before going their separate ways, Nelish quickly loads a tracking beacon into Dominic's shooting device and focuses his target directly on the center of the lead panther's back.

"Gotcha!" Nelish whisper, as he fires the sharp-pointed tracking device. "Swhoop," is the sound of the tracking device as it was released and wisped through the air, effortlessly penetrating the fur into the guard's back.

Nelish and Dominic quickly return to cover as the lead panther rubbed his shoulder and shouts, "Whoa, I guess the mosquitoes are pretty busy tonight!" He is unaware of what had actually just taken place as he leads the other panther guards and the captives away. While the remaining panther guards performs final patrols around the area in efforts of finding stragglers, Nelish and Dominic quietly flew away and returns to Dominic's hideout.

Dominic loaded the signal coordinates into his reception device. He informs Nelish that the receptor will continue to provide an accurate signal of the captives' whereabouts as soon as they reach their destination. Dominic states, "When the detector produces a sound, this will confirm where the captives are." "Thanks for the encouragement, Dominic. You have been truly magnificent during these rough patches. I'm sorry we had to meet this way," Nelish said gingerly as he waits for the tracking device to provide a confirmation sound. "Better to meet this way, Nelish, then to not have met you at all." -Dominic sincerely replies.

Nelish thought of a plan to rescue his parents. He said his thoughts aloud, "Moments ago, we were outnumbered by the large panthers out there. We have to outsmart them, should we have to face them head on. We must somehow use stealth in order to rescue my parents and all of the captives. Are you up for the challenge, Dominic? This is not your battle, and it was not my intention to put you through all of this danger. I would completely understand if you cannot continue, because you've helped me well enough!"

Dominic states, "Your fight is my fight, senor! You've rescued me when I haven't asked, so I now help you fight the good fight too, without asking, my amigo!"

Nelish smiles as he gives Dominic a high five. "Okay then, my friend," Nelish began. "Here's how we are going to rescue the others! Since we are outnumbered, we need to balance our attacks. What I mean is, we can even our fighting chances by making some firepower. We need to plant some explosives throughout the area where the predators are."

"Right!" Dominic states. "I can create multiple grenades, and the detonations could definitely benefit us by causing major chaos and distractions while the captives are freed, but we need a diversion."

"Indeed!" Nelish begin, and then continues, "I can cause a diversion by appearing directly in the enemies' line of sight. Then, Dominic, since you are the expert at making arsenals, while you stealthily place the explosives in the target areas, I'll make sure to be the life of the party!"

"I'm getting right to it!" Dominic eagerly states as he begins processing the grenades. Suddenly the detector sounds. Nelish pause at the sudden confirmation. "Wow." Dominic cheers. Target: *Panthron*! Immediately, a focused look was set upon Nelish's face as he balled his feathered fist together. With a determined look in his eye, he states, "To *Panthron* we shall go!"

Meanwhile, the panthers arrive at Parag's fortress and present the new captives to Parag. The captives are tied together while their mouths are covered only being able to look around. "Aww, more visitors requesting my permission to stay? Well, of course you are welcome to! I am honored by your request. You are by far too kind. I do get rather lonely at times, and too much company is never enough!" Parag said with amusement. "Oh by the way, don't anyone try to be clever and try to find a way out, my dear newfound friends. The last couple, two peacocks to be exact, tried to proclaim a bargain. In exchange, they received an unwanted early dismal...of no way out! I would rather not do such a thing. I cannot tolerate disloyalty! So please, enjoy your stay! Guards," Parag calls slyly, "As your reward, I will allow you to receive the pleasures of their loyalty by serving you and obeying your commands. This is a token of my gratitude to you, my brothers!"

"Indeed, Parag!" the panther guards respectfully reply.

Parag seldom shared captives with the lower guards, but every so often, he rewards them by releasing captives over to them to perform services, in exchange for the guards' acts of obedience. The panthers laugh. "Now we can take a break from our rendezvous and rest easy!" One of the guards loosened the ropes and order the captives to fan and massage them, as they unwound and rest. Other captives are led to the food chambers and receive orders to provide food to the panthers and feed them. As these activities took place in the background, Parag watches as the captives steadily continues assembling his statue and other collections. While being fanned by captives, Parag proclaims, as Mahato is mercilessly chained nearby to bear witness, "Now all of Bangladesh will respect the reign of the panthers, under my authority," Parag proudly stated. "I will not rest until the panthers are the number one mascot of Bangladesh!"

The Plan

Prior to arriving to Bangladesh, Nelish thought it's best to find some leverage that would allow them to defend themselves against the predators. Since the panthers are greater in size and stature, he determines it is better to have a backup plan for defense which includes firepower. For this, Dominic created dynamite. As the dynamite was finished, Dominic thought it's best to set them in key areas, so as they erupted, the explosions would cause chain reactions and allow the surrounding areas to combust, without the impact of disrupting the other nearby dynamite. This would save the remaining dynamite for other areas to deploy separately. Nelish determine that while the dynamite blasts will cause distractions to the surrounding guards, it would be the ideal opportunity to rescue the captives, however many they may be. Ultimately, Nelish's goal is to join Dominic, meet up with Mahato and all captives, as well as reunite with his parents once more.

Panthron (Parag's Fortress)

Nelish leads the way as the team flew in together with the help of the tracking device. Without conflict or any alert, they successfully land in the heart of Bangladesh, where they witness the beauty of the diverse greenery, rivers, lakes, and mountainous terrain. The beauty is truly a sight to behold, yet they remain focus on their objective at hand. They knew that the land is highly secure by their opposition and there is certainly no time to waste to enjoy the natural wonders.

"We are here!" Dominic whispers.

"Finally, after all this time, it comes down to this. The land of Bangladesh, where life began for me, as I've been told. I have not lived here because of my parents' fear of the opposition. We escaped years ago. I've arrived at my birthplace, yet I know so little of it. I have many questions about it, but now my focus is to reunite with my family, and that could be settled during a later discussion," Nelish whispers.

"We're getting closer to their position senor," Dominic whispers.

"Great, we will soon split apart to complete our objectives," Nelish whispers. They position themselves for a more suitable stealthy approach, hiding within the vines and other higher trees above ground. As they laid over the surface, their attention centers on the activity beneath them. They hear laughter and other commotion carrying on. "Keep moving prey! Your master patiently awaits the completion of his honor!"-shouts a panther guard. "Press harder!"-shout another predator. They notice the panther guards standing in various positions patrolling certain job assigned areas, while others patrol to guard against fleeing captives.

Nelish and Dominic saw the captives actively engaging in assembling a statue, which appears to be the adorning of a panther. Everywhere captives are constantly performing different activities to appease Parag. In the distance, Mahato was spotted, chained and separated from the rest. Nelish could do nothing as he remain in cover, staring at the continuous activity. "There!" Nelish whispered. He continued by stating, "There's our great leader and founder of our village, Mahato!" "He looks helpless, while he is under chains!" "He has done so much for us." "We must free him!" Nelish states this, while witnessing the sweat pouring across the captives' faces, the dreariness of their composure, the lack of sleep that glaze their eyes, and the countless efforts to please the guards, even while maintaining their composure. He notices the insults of the panther guards as they constantly taunt the captives and impose their influence over them.

Nelish is not pleased as he whispers to Dominic, "The panthers will pay for this indeed!"

"Soon they shall," Dominic whispers back as he looks over the scene as the action unfold.

Suddenly, Parag appears. As he approaches to oversee the laborers, Nelish lays eyes upon him for the first time. Parag's servants made way for him as he continued to his throne.

"That's him!" Nelish whispers.

"Ha, ha, ha! Excellent, my servants! I am well pleased with your progress thus far!" Parag said excitedly.

"I remember that laughter!" Nelish's mind quickly flood with memories of what led to this, of being separated from his family. "He was the leader of the charge that captured my parents and brought them here!" Nelish whispers. "Now, Dominic, this is the best opportunity for you to assemble the explosives."

"Agreed!" Dominic whispers. "Nelish, here is the detonator which will control the explosives. I'll give you the signal at the right moment! Best of luck to you, my friend." The captives worked as they continue receiving commands, force to carrying out their various tasks and other assignments.

As Nelish and Dominic stealthily went their separate ways, Parag utters, "Yes, my servants. The crowning achievement of my statue is truly coming together. It's been many moons I've awaited this day, and it was well worth the wait! Ha, ha, ha! Don't fret my loyal subjects. I understand your burden, as I too am excited to see the completion of my image. I know you've toiled and been suppressed by the intense climate, oh you poor dears!" Parag said sarcastically. "Soon, you will be able to receive a well-deserved rest. You have tirelessly tried to please me, and I highly commend you for that. More water please," he then says to a servant.

As the servant approaches Parag, Nelish notices that the servant look oddly familiar. Thoughts began processing in Nelish's mind, and eventually became clear: it was the captive that had laid eyes on him while being carried away by the panther guards, the female Sarus Crane. She is a beauty to lay eyes upon and Nelish becomes a little more agitated once the servant girl appear with an elegant pitcher while delicately pouring water into Parag's glass. He realizes that he has to keep his composure, or the whole rescue plan would fail. "Thanks, darling," Parag said, as she smartly carried on her way, away from him. Nelish is more determine, even now, to rescue the captives. The hope of seeing and reuniting with his parents' again, burns deeply inside of him.

As Dominic distances himself from Nelish, he is determining to set up the dynamite. He knows his objective far too well, which is to install the explosive in key areas throughout Parag's fortress and create a diversion for the guards. The guards constantly patrol the area, so he understands that he has to be swift and keen to detail, or else the plan would fail. Dominic lands safely behind more plants and shrubbery. He surveys the surrounding area, searching for the best points to place the bombs. He calculates the radius and how a single detonation should actually combine to create another explosion and spread the dynamite to other areas. He dodges panther guards by blending into surrounded areas, awaiting guards to shift their focus deterred, or simply by flying over them. As Dominic flies and plants dynamite, it was one area in particular he knew that Nelish would be pleased for him to do so. Dominic knows it's already a tedious task to stealthily assemble dynamite in the open while avoiding predators. Now he faces actually trying to assemble the dynamite on Parag's statue while construction is currently going on. The statue featuring Parag's body was completely assembled, so now they are assembling the head. Dominic notices the captives are working steadily, so thought it will be best not to be spotted under such circumstances. So he plans to place the dynamite upon an extended object and launch it from afar to avoid detection. He places the dynamite inside the form of a plunger, with the rubber end facing forward and the time bomb attachment hanging from inside the middle. Dominic disguised the bomb with leaves and other plants to make it appear as a tunnel of leaves tangled together, thus trying to not alert the guards that anything had actually occurred. As planned, Dominic sizes up the target into his enhanced binoculars and once the target was acquired, he covertly fired the shot along with the attachment onto the back of the panther statue. "Picture perfect!" Dominic whispers as the disguised bomb went unrecognized. The captives continued assembling the statue, unaware of anything that had just taken place. Dominic, from a distance, signals Nelish with feathered thumbs up, indicating the installment process is complete. Finally, as discussed, the bombs were set up in key areas, and it is now up to Nelish to go forward as planned.

The Moment of Truth

Parag is thoroughly pleased as he ceremoniously appears before his audience and watched as the assembling of his statue nears completion. "My loyal servants, come forth!" He orders the captives that serve him as personal assistants to appear before him. As they did, one of the servants is the same familiar Sarus Crane that Nelish had seen before. Nelish saw the glow in her eye as she notices that Nelish is nearby from the corner of her eye. Nelish witnesses her once more from above, and it appears as if she knows he is observing the events taking place, probably because she is involve throughout the process, and the fact that she is a female. Perhaps she is astonished that he was on a rescue mission and was yet to be caught. Witnessing her behavior, Nelish feels that by her actions she seems to be leading him on to something as if she is trying to aid him in his heroic efforts and continued to play along with being a captive for now, moving forward with the others to Parag to perform his requests.

He orders a few servants to fully assemble his robe, staff, and quickly make way, clean around his presence, and promptly roll out a royal elegant carpet before him. He immediately summon a few panther guards to remain behind and secure the captives while he allow higher ranking others to attend as witnesses to behold his glorious event while leaving a few behind to remain at their posts. The panther guards that attended the ceremony upon Parag's request gather around him.

Ceremoniously Parag states, "Behold, the crowning achievement of my success, rendered from the allegiance of the tiger kingdom, in which I am indeed greatly honored to reign supreme in the land of Bangladesh upon the throne of Panthron! I served honorably by possessing the land, as I loyally proclaimed the dominance of the (Panther) Claw Association. My brothers, bear witness with me now as it is revealed to you that the panther nation has come to pass. This statue is a tribute to our rule, wherein other predators pale in comparison and are no longer among us but beneath us. I'm sure they are thirsty to challenge us, but we are relentless and while allow none other to interfere with our establishment! Our prey, as you witness this moment, will continue to be loyal servants to us as we continue to reign here as mascots of this land and onward! Ha, ha, ha! Fellow brothers, let's pay homage to our loyal servants now, by giving them our undivided attention and respect as they mount the crowning jewel, my replica, and fully complete "The Statue of Prominence." My statue is a sight to behold, as I have dearly entitled the name to be!" Parag said pompously. The panther audience and special guests publically laughs, cheers, and awaited the decree of the statue's finalization. Nelish, witness the moment of truth and finally realize why Parag assembled the efforts of capturing prey throughout the land. After beholding Parag's true objective, Nelish states to himself, "I finally see what Parag's true attempts are. To capture my village and make them as prey servants forcing them to submit to his high predator rule and hail him and his forces as mascots of this land!" Nelish eyes grows more intently and the more focus and aware he became. While gathering his attempt to strike, he envisions his parents' teachings. Nelish questions himself by stating, "Could this be my true purpose, to battle forces with the merciless Parag?" The moment arise as confidence builds inside him. Nelish passionately responds, "Surely this moment is what mother expressed to me about!"

Out of nowhere, suddenly a glistening sharp spear-like object struck the earth and remained there, nearly missing Parag... as Nelish dashes to the scene, dramatically appearing from the distance into plain sight.

"There will be no crowning jewels today!" Nelish states loudly. The moment of truth began when Nelish knew he had to create a diversion to allow Dominic time to release the captives. As planned, Nelish appears before Parag. Sharply, Parag turns to see the individual who had courage enough to utter such statements before him while awaiting the completion of his statue. The audience gasped aloud. "How dare you utter such words in my presence?!" "Who are you?!"

"My name is Nelish the Peacock!" Nelish said boldly, taking a heroic stance as the wind sail through his plumage, causing an epic appearance. "Not now or ever shall this day of commencement occur!" Nelish boldly proclaims, stiffly pointing at Parag. As Nelish squares off with Parag, Dominic stealthily maneuvers in the background; trying to free nearby captives. Dominic whispers to himself, as he relentlessly searches throughout covert spaces to gain access to various captives. "Okay, Dominic!" Don't let Nelish down! "You have to blaze past these guards and rescue your familia!" "Goodness, I see guards everywhere! What's a bird to do?!!! "Oh yes, I have seafood delicacies, by which I can lure the guards of their posts to obtain them." Thinking in deep thought, Dominic ponder options, "Hmmmmm, let me see!" "What do we have here?" "Shrimp and sleeping spices should do the trick!" Dominic quickly unleashes various amounts of seafood and loads it with sleepy fibers disguised as spices. While mixing them together he replies, "I'm very disappointed in giving up my favorite food to satisfy mi appetite, but I'm sure these predators will deserve this delicioso delicacy far more!" "Voila!" "I'm such a genuioso!" "Now to distract the guards and free the captives!" While continuing to avoid panther guards, Dominic sights a few captives preparing food in response from the guard's commands. "Perfect!" Dominic states, as he hastily appears before the captives. Unaware of Dominic's arrival, the captives continue to prepare the guards' meals while suddenly Dominic appears. "Shh!" He whispers. "I'm here to free you. But first, before you hand them their dishes, add this *special* shrimp to their food and be sure to give it to all of them. Inside it is a sleeping substance that will momentarily tire the guards. Once asleep, I will be able to free all of you!" Hope fills the captives eyes and they eagerly offer the prepare meals to the guards. Knowing that the Parag was moments away from receiving the crowning achievement, the panther guards were a little relaxed from their usual straightforward duties while serving their posts. "Dinner is served." –States a captive. "Mmmmmhhh!" "Looks delicious, some of the guards sounded!" "Wow, let me at this shrimp!" "We definitely are glad you prey are here to serve us." Slurping and eagerly eating their meals, the panther guards' reply- "We will definitely keeping you captives around longer!" "It's been a long time overdue with Parag's offerings to us!" "Leave us now and prepare more!" "As you wish, another captive responds, as they carry food to all the remaining guards. The panther guards heavily dine in on their gratifying meal. "Wow!" "This meal was delicious! Various guards express while returning to their areas. Now, I may just take a quick catnap to refocus."- Others state as well. Moments later, the guards grew tired and slump over their posts. "Now it's our chance familia, show me were the remaining captives are and let's get out of here! Pronto!" Dominic proclaimed. "We must remain quiet and alert in case there are other guards that may be on patrol." He quietly told them to remain calm until he finishes freeing them. He also alerts them that the panther guards the might still be lurking around.

Amazed at the heroic appearance of Nelish the Peacock, Parag seems flattered and amused of his persistence to face the likes of him. Everyone in attendance--the panther guards, official guests, captives, and Parag--paused to bear witness to the situation. "Hmmmmm!" "The classic analogy."-"Predator versus Prey!" "Why even bother?" "For we all knows who wins.....don't we?" Parag questioned Nelish further. "Do you think that I will allow a mere peacock stop me from enjoying my day? You're just a peacock, the least of any threat! "Hmmmm, I'm sure I heard that before." Nelish states. Parag counters and sarcastically replies, "I've faced countless lesser predators fiercer than you, and you dare to defy me?! Ha, ha, ha! You are not even worth the time of me scarring a claw to retrieve you N-e-l-i-s-h, you mellishing peacock!" Parag proudly lifts his forepaw as he turns his back on Nelish. "You may continue to watch me, as I proceed to receive my well-deserved honor, which is far overdue I might add, and you shall be the first to kneel in respect of me!" Parag states this as he intentionally proceeds to continue on with the procession as though Nelish wasn't standing there. "Behold, now... My servants, continue forward!" Parag screamed. "Afterward, you shall prepare a dish for me, lad, as my number one servant!" Parag continues.

"Perhaps I didn't make myself clear!" Nelish states, while holding the detonator behind his back. He firmly looks squarely into the eyes of Parag. Nelish's eyes become laser focused and determined, as his demeanor was poised and positioned to strike at any moment.

Parag scowls at Nelish and becomes even more frustrated. Thoughts enters his mind, and is made bitter by the fact that he had awaited his whole ambitious career to receive such an honor, and now his most ceremonious moment is ruined. He tries to maintain a straight face. He is not use to anyone undermining him, especially during formal events. "If it's me you want, then it's me you shall have!"-Nelish stated.

"Release them now and no one will get hurt!" Nelish yells.

"Ha, ha, ha, and how would you do such a thing, oh noble one? I do admire your courage, I really do, but you see, that is an impossible feat to accomplish, dear one. What a pity, it seems as if you had your whole life ahead of you, until now," Parag says with sarcastic sadness. He continues, "Defenses are set everywhere and you are surrounded by everyone! You have no way out! Give up now and let's pretend this minor mishap never occurred. Will you?" Parag slyly laughs. All witness the confrontation between Nelish and Parag, as they wonders what will happen next. "Anything else you would like to wish, before we continue forward?" Parag expresses.

While all the attention was placed on Nelish and Parag, Dominic suddenly appears in the distance, unharmed. He motion to Nelish that he was clear to detonate the bombs. After receiving assurance from Dominic that the captives are freed, unknown to Parag or the panther guards, Nelish eagerly says, "Before we leave here today, I wish to see my parents and no one will get hurt!"

"Parents? Why, Nelish, is that what this commotion was all about? If you wanted to see your parents, you could have just asked instead of causing all of this unbearable trouble." Parag laughs.

Immediately, Parag mentally calculates that Nelish's urgent arrival was to rescue the very same couple that he had assassinated. Instead of complying with Nelish's wish, after putting two and two together, he determined by Nelish's assuredness that he was caught in a trap. Buying some time to think upon the matter, Parag express, "Hmmmmm, it seems that some sort of diversion has taken place! You seem a little too assure of yourself." In response to recognizing a distraction must have taken place, Parag immediately cries out, "Guards, attack!"

"Too late!" Nelish jeered. In an instant, Nelish pressed the detonator button behind his back. Immediately, the detonator simultaneously set off dynamite, causing the explosive disruption. The outbursts cause chaos everywhere. Instantly Parag focus his attention upon Nelish, while the surrounding predators flee for cover. The moment left Parag and Nelish, centered squarely upon each other, as boulders and surrounding items dismantles around them. Laser focused, Parag unsheathes his claws and began pacing circular motions around Nelish. Assessing the situation, Parag tries zeroing in on Nelish in efforts to find closure by stating, "So, you think you've won this battle?" "NEVER!" "I'm just getting started to be annoyed with you, just a little!" "I have toyed with you enough!" "Temper, temper there Parag!" Nelish heroically stated, while positioning into a defensive counter stance; awaiting for Parag attacks. "Now peacock, this is where all good things come to an end, and it starts with you!" Without hesitation, Parag performs a swiping motion within inches of Nelish face. Folding inward as if was trying to brace for cover, suddenly Nelish counters by folding his wings and then outstretching them in return with an object. "Clink!" The sound provides, as Nelish shields himself while blocking Parag's attacks with his hardened feather blades. "What manner of defense is this?!" Parag cries aloud. "No matter, I will still crush the likes of you as I have performed with countless others!" "Clink, clink,

clink," as the sounds grew louder as Parag tried to provide multiple attacks. "Stay still Peacock!" "I want to see what makes you tick!" Nelish continue to block Parag's attacks with his feather-blades, as well as ducked and dodged multiple strikes. Confident that he's effectively countering, Nelish replies "Wow, Parag! I'm starting to say that I'm getting a little bored of your tactics!" "Very well Peacock! I will make a swift exit of you and proceed to carry on like you never exist! Parag snarls while attempting to strike yet again. "Close but no cigar!"-Nelish states as he continues to counter Parag's swipes. Parag's failed attempts cause further destruction as he trampled items all over his fortress trying to dispel of Nelish. Nelish ducks and dodges Parag strikes as he leaps into his personal treasures and furniture. Momentarily able to provide closing arguments as Parag attempts to regain composure, Nelish proclaims, "Today, my village family and surrounding victims are no longer oppressed by the likes of you and your kind!" He continues on, as the earth gave way underneath them. "Look around Parag, your paradise is lost and my friends are no longer bound by predator rule! "No!" Parag yelled. "My captives! My livelihood! My glorious moment shall not be ruined in such a manner as this!" Suddenly Nelish and Parag were momentarily separated from each other. "It's over Parag!" "All of your failed attempts to hail as Bangladesh's mascot are final!" "Your guards and guests have left for cover!" "Save your dignity and yourself while you are ahead." Nelish proclaim.

Meanwhile, Dominic led the captives to freedom through the eruptions, avoiding the rocky debris as it flew everywhere. The captives notify Dominic that their chief leader Mahato is held captive elsewhere. "Thanks for saving us!" One of the elders cry out, "But we must save our village leader and chief, Mahato! He has done so much for us, and we are not worthy to leave besides him!" "He is currently held captive in a specific area!" Dominic hurriedly replies, "Your familia! Mi familia as well!" "Show me where he is!" The village elders, led by Dominic, and the freed captives' race among treacherous debris; narrowing their escape to free Mahato, the more. "There he is cries one of the elders." The impact of the separation of Parag's fortress is disturbingly separating Dominic from reaching Mahato. "Save yourself and the others!" Mahato states from afar. "I am at peace seeing my villagers saved!" Knowing that he had a certain amount of time left, last but not least, he leaves the freed captives and flew in to rescue Mahato from his chains, just in the nick of time, by using special gadgetry to release him. "Hi familia! No….Dominic's here to rescue you!" "Hold on tight!" "We will get you out!" Mahato acknowledged by implying yes, as Dominic unravels the chains around him. Dominic states, it's certainly a pleasure to meet you senor! I heard so many great things about you, but definitely outside of these circumstances!" Dominic place an unlocking mechanism among the chains, causing them to loosen its grip once he activate a deactivating signal. "Voila!" Dominic states. Freedom and relief engulfes Mahato, as Dominic frees him. "I knew this day would come, thank you!" - Mahato stated, as he tried to regain his composure and posture, after being chained; for such a long period of time. "Right this way senor!" Dominic hastily states, as he ushers Mahato and the freed villagers to safety. The ground gave way where Mahato was imprisoned. Fully alerted now the panther guards regain their attention and composure. "The captives, we must obtain the captives!" Shouts a panther guard. "We must save ourselves!", shouts another panther guard. "The explosions are far too great and everything is crumbling beneath us!" "I'm out of here!"-sounded others. Debris contaminants dispel, prompting the panther guards and special guests to become wounded, distracted, and had no clue of what to do next. The ignition caused a dynamo effect, which created earthquakes and fault lines everywhere. As the earth opened beneath them, they avoided that too in their search for safety.

Parag express outrage as he witnesses the calamity unfolding throughout his domain. He bear witness to see the end result as his nearly assembled statue crumbling into a heap before his eyes. As the destruction continues, Parag set his sights again upon Nelish. Maneuvering around the shattering and tremendous quakes, suddenly he is able to return to steady ground. "Peacock, I've underestimated you severely and because of this, you indeed unveil a chink in my armor. Since you provided a lasting imprint on me, in return--since I am far too generous as well--I want to provide you something of lasting importance, which will leave you far more devastated." Nelish's attention span focused upon those words as he listens intently as Parag to his very words. Parag begins to caress his chin as if in wonder as he begin his statement of rhetorical questions, "Today, I lost precious memorabilia, but's what's more precious than reputation? "Hmmmm...." "Perhaps, riches?" "Perhaps, fame?" "Perhaps, members of one's family." "Hmmmm." "Let me see...."-as Parag ponders those thoughts." "I believe the latter spells it all."-Parag smartly follows up. Suddenly the moment of truth arose as Parag focuses on Nelish. At a distance while squarely looking into Nelish's face, he states "As you lay your eyes upon mine, you've placed your eyes upon the one who killed your beloved parents!" Parag snickered.

Hearing those words was a penetrating blow to Nelish. His eyes grew in disbelief, as he was startled and begun to lose focus of what took place around him. He was speechless and crushed the moment he heard them.

Prior to hearing those words, Nelish plan to escape along with Dominic and the captives, but now he face such shocking news. Parag knew the news will cause a distracting, freezing Nelish's judgment instantly, allowing him to strike during his most vulnerable moment. As the destruction and chaos continues, Nelish and Parag are completely isolated from everyone. Parag took that opportunity to destroy the very one he had taken for granted while focusing on his crowning achievement. He momentarily felt that this victory would heal the hurt and embarrassment he faces. Sullen, Nelish is vulnerable to Parag's strike as the panther bolts toward him. Concentrated and determined, Parag launches forward into the air and positions himself for the perfect strike. While in midair, he pulls his forearm back for a powerful swipe and swiftly lunges for Nelish.

Suddenly, Parag's attempted fatal blow is disrupted by a former captive, aiming for his eyes, which was the Sarus Crane that Nelish had encountered twice along the way. There was no time to lose as Parag awkwardly fumbles, trying to regain his sight. Causing Parag to be distracted, the Sarus Crane quickly pulls Nelish away from Parag's area, as she tries to refocus Nelish's attention and get him to fly for cover. Nelish immediately wakes up from his sullen mood and responds to the Sarus Crane's efforts. As he did so, Parag regains his sight and tries to recover his failed attempt. While the Sarus Crane's position was toward Nelish, as she was making sure of his awareness, Parag reappears. While unaware that Parag suddenly appears, he saw that the Sarus Crane's attention is on Nelish and this made her rear vulnerable to Parag. Parag used this as another opportunity to strike at them both. Parag pounces in their direction at full stride.

Nelish, fully alert and aware of Parag's intentions, immediately swipes the Sarus Crane away, jumping on top of her and rolling them away from the vicious strike. Distraught and unnerved, Parag states, "Nelish the Peacock, you've haven't scratched the surface of defeating me!" Once they recover, they had just barely flown away when Parag tried one last attempt to strike at them. Immediately, Nelish counters by thwarting several feathered daggers at him, "Clink", forcing one of his paws to momentarily remain steadfast upon the ground. Nelish heroically states as he's accompanied by the Sarus Crane. "Don't mellish with Nelish!" Parag screamed as they flew away. "You may have gotten away this time, but you haven't seen the last of me, Nelish the Peacock!"

More and more, the debris scattered and caused ripple effects. Rocks raced downward, causing them to appear as granite hailstorms. Ashes and smoke billowed, blackening the view. Parag watches the remains of his once towering statue fall, and loudly proclaims, "Nelish the Peacock!" Parag ran for cover as the effects of the destruction spread.

*****story break*****

Nelish and Dominic's objective was to free the captives from Parag's fortress. Although the stakes were high in the recovery efforts, the objectives had been achieved according to plan, for the most part until Nelish had discovered the shocking truth of his parents' whereabouts. Although his primary motive was to rescue and reunite with his parents, he had instead developed friendships and restored hope to the captives, created enemies, and developed a sure sense of inner confidence and self-worth. A true hero was born, while a sacrifice was made that led to the other's death.

*****story resume*****

Meanwhile, Dominic leads the former captives away from Parag's fortress and to an undisclosed location where they could remain hidden from predator forces. "Thank you Dominic the flamingo and special thanks to Nelish as well! Soon I shall meet him and honor him for such bravery and heroic efforts." Afterwards, Mahato rests, as he tries to regain strength from the persecution he faced. The freed villagers thanks gracefully Dominic for his rescuing efforts, and informs him of the many tortures they've faced while captive there. Dominic thanked them for their courage in remaining vigilant. He stated that his rescue efforts had paled in comparison to the situations they had faced, saying they were the real heroes. "You guys are the real heroes. You faced and conquered misery while standing tall through the midst of trouble; Thanks to Nelish for believing in us and in himself." "Now fellow friends, you are free to remain here until Nelish arrives to ensure your safety. He should return momentarily."

As Nelish heads back to join Dominic, Mahato and the freed captives, the Sarus Crane stops Nelish mid-flight and motioned for him to pause. They land nearby to talk. Looking around, Nelish cautiously surveys the area to see if any predators are around. "Seems like we are pretty clear, I should say," Nelish states. Afterwards, he looks off into the distance, as he wonders if his rescue efforts had been in vain. He remains silent as the wind swiftly travels through his feathers.

Respectfully understanding the situation Nelish is in, the Sarus Crane proceeds forward, as if to provide comforting words by saying, "Thanks for saving everyone, as well as I, back there. Rescuing us was very heroic of you and your friend, performing such a feat, not knowing that you would fly out of there alive. Being captured by the enemy, that was definitely not one of my most proud moments." The Sarus Crane giggled sheepishly.

"No need to thank me. I wanted to make sure that everyone was saved, well, almost everyone." Nelish continue to stare off into the distance.

Heartfelt and moved by Nelish's reply, the Sarus Crane slowly approaches Nelish and gracefully stood in front of him as she joins her feathered hands with his. "Nelish," she said calmly, "You did what you thought was right in your heart, by searching for your family. You did all you could have possibly done." The Sarus Crane continues, "If anyone could succeed in a rescue mission, I knew that one would be you. By the way, the name's Ruby. You put on quite a performance back there and you definitely made a believer in me. I admire your skills, because I too believe in accepting the challenge of defending myself, although I was clearly outnumbered. I should not have allowed myself to be captured and placed into this predicament in the first place," Ruby replies, scolding herself.

"No need to blame yourself," Nelish said, looking into Ruby's darling eyes. His eyes glistened as if the sun shone upon them. The surrounding wind races the more as they stare into each other's eyes. "As if you didn't know, I'm Nelish the Peacock, and I do apologize for meeting you in this manner. If I could, I would have clearly done things differently!" Nelish appears to smirk a little as he applies a lttle humor to soften his emotional wounds.

"I never had a chance to meet your parents, but it seems as if they are been extremely proud of your efforts today," Ruby warmly states.

"Indeed, Ruby, and it would have been an honor for them to have met you." "I can imagine them embracing you now." "Well mother perhaps anyway." Nelish smiles. Wondering how she alone had spotted him several times while in cover, he asked, "By the way, how did you know it was I that attempted to rescue all of you?" Ruby answers slyly, "It's a woman's secret you know, and as a female warrior at that, she can't reveal all of her secrets, can she?"

Nelish smiles in return and adds, "That makes two of us! Thanks for saving me as well back there! Let's join the others!" "I'm sure they waited long enough!" Nelish states as he positions Dominic's whereabouts on his GPS tracker and they flew away to join him and the others.

*****story break*****

Ruby the Sarus Crane

About Ruby the Sarus Crane's existence is not fully known, but it is believed that she was born of a middle class family from the land of India. Abandoned, due to predator run-ins, she was force to independently survive on her own. While being self-taught, she believes in defending herself and is somewhat of a vigilante.

Ruby is a competitive female that enjoys having fun. She is a weapons expert and enjoys utilizing other gizmos and gadgets. She is ambitious and admires challenges that come along the way. She is also witty, agile, stealthy, and aggressive.

While her past remains a mystery, though, she has a personal vendetta to settle, with members of any opposition. While Ruby remains loyal to defending prey, defenseless and other targeted animals, she can be listed as something of a wild card, as she seeks to attack the opposition and settle personal scores. While this may be honorable, the same behavior may also lead to unnecessary trouble. Ruby obtained her name from the fact that she is skilled at collecting items, hence the name "Ruby." It also validates the fact that she loves treasure, possibly meaning it's something she may have always desired but didn't have the means of obtaining in the past. In conclusion, Ruby is a mysterious yet likeable character, because she is loyal. Yet there lies intrigue within her, and don't double-cross her. Maintaining a warrior's mentality, Ruby is fully capable of tangoing with the opposition.

Finally, Nelish and Ruby meets up with Dominic, Mahato, and the freed captives. "We are here!" Nelish responds. Dominic races up to embrace Nelish and greets Ruby. "Yay you did it Nelish!- Dominic happily states. "No, we did it Dominic!"- Nelish replies as they embrace once more. Soon after, Nelish looks upon Mahato and his villagers. Graciously Nelish steps forward to a resting Mahato as he shows reverence to his stature and provides smiles to the on-looking villagers. Mahato re-gathers his composure, realizing Nelish is present, as he prepares to honor Nelish. "Thank you for your valiant efforts Nelish." "You are truly indeed a warrior at heart and I sincerely admire your spirit!" As a lad, you were always unique with astounding charisma. I know your father wanted you to be of a different mold, but your very same uniqueness was the very foundation that brought us together again, which we are forever grateful." "It indeed saddens me of our loss but I'm sure your parents are very proud of such a rare and genuine marvel you are!" "I understand that the foundation of our community and our people are of one spirit, one peace, but the heroic efforts of you and your friends, prove to be valiant and has caught my attention!" "Predators constantly seek approval amongst the ranks in order to remain on top of the food chain, and they will not rest." "But thanks be to you, words cannot express how truly I feel about you, but for now, we will save that for another day." Nelish, touched by the reception of those words of gladness, returns the gratitude to Mahato by expressing, "Thank you Chief Mahato!" "I don't have all the answers right now as to my reasons for bravery, but it was your courage and strength to unify us as a village which set the primary example for us to follow - I believe." "I just wanted to see you all again by giving everything I had, thanks to my friends I met along the way!" - Nelish respectfully states. Nelish continues, "Chief Mahato, how do we return to our village? Mahato laughs,

"Nelish, although I've spent countless amounts of days orchestrating Malihayah as one community, the true and simple fact is, to understand that we are the community. The village can certainly be replaced, but we cannot. We are the value and the community spirit of togetherness lies in you!" Dominic replies, I'm sure I will be able to handle the rebuilding efforts. No problem!-"Well, respectively with your permission first of course senior. Dominic states as he gracefully bows in respect to Mahato's decision. "Dominic, wherever we settle next, you are always invited to join us! The villagers laugh in response. The elders embrace the villagers as they provide comfort to them, informing them that they survive such a great ordeal of battle. Noticing Mahato was separated from his sacred paradise he provided as a safe haven unto all prey refugees, Nelish politely asks, "How do you presently feel now Chief Mahato?" Mahato wisely states, "My inner strength is strong, but my physical strength currently needs recharging." "For now, we dine and celebrate reuniting!" "For surely tomorrow brings forth new challenges!"

Meanwhile, in the land of Bangladesh, as the darkness settled and the chaos cleared, Parag arose out of the ashes. Cunning as before, never baffled and never admitting defeat, he appears proud and amused yet again as he summon forth his brotherhood Parag promptly states, "Panther-hood, arise out of the ashes, I beseech thee. For it seems as if we have been ushered into an era where members beneath my prestige have quite the courage. A courage, I've never seen before. Just know that such a battle has suddenly taken place. Countless times, I have surpassed the opposition without question and become quite bored with winning and seamlessly achieved triumph. But finally, I feel rejuvenated and thirsty for oppressing the opposition and putting forth an effort to wipe out such nonsense once and for all! It appears that my providence has been dismantled by unruly guests, but there's nothing to throw a fit about. It seems we actually have to think on how to outwit our competitors. The forthcoming battles will be quite interesting for a change. Nonetheless, we are the mascots of Bangladesh, and no one, I mean no one, not predator, nor prey, shall take what we own!" I will not rest until I have complete control! "Guards!" Parag shouted, "Assemble the scavengers together! I need spies to search out the encampment throughout, and proclaim that they should search for the pheasant which proclaims himself as Nelish the Peacock!"

Closeout

This concludes Nelish Daring Quests, Book 1. Stay tuned for further quests that include Nelish the Peacock.

About the Author

Kevin David Grant began drawing at the tender age of 5. Realizing he was blessed with creative talents in writing and spending countless of years in drawing, he received sound advice from his immediate family members as well as his high school senior English teacher, (Barbara Delac), to shoot for the stars with his special gifts. He intentionally had ideas of going to an art college to fulfill his dream, but life simply wasn't easy paying for college tuition for a single individual, let alone a teenage kid, especially when you are 1 of 3 triplet men graduating high school at the same time- which he is! Instead, he decided to join the military, in efforts of serving his country around the world, in return for education benefits by enrolling into a college of his choice. Although serving in the U.S. Navy for over 12 years, obtaining a family, and successfully obtaining a Bachelor's of Science of Organizational Management Degree from the University of LaVerne in 2012, he was happy of those accomplishments, but yet he felt emptiness inside and was still unsatisfied. Although life happened and time passed by, he still had the passion and the desire to pursue and fulfill his lifelong dream of providing quality entertainment for all. He decided to combine both his imagination and artwork compiled together into a book, and Nelish Daring Quests was birth forth. Finally he feels that he is putting his imagination at work, and with your efforts, his dreams will successfully be a reality. This is his gift to the world! Embrace it…

"Life is precious, but it's rare and even more precious when you are born as a multiple, triplets to be exact!" - Kevin D. Grant

Made in the USA
Lexington, KY
29 August 2018